Jennifer Jones Won't Leave Me Alone

For my friend, Phoebe Gilman – F.W.
For Gabriel and Apple, with thanks to Dr Hok – N.L.

JENNIFER JONES WON'T LEAVE ME ALONE
A PICTURE CORGI BOOK 978 0 552 57302 3

First published in Great Britain by Doubleday,
an imprint of Random House Children's Books
A Random House Group Company
Doubleday edition published 2003
Picture Corgi edition published 2004
This edition published 2012
1 3 5 7 9 10 8 6 4 2
Text copyright © Frieda Wishinsky, 2003
Illustrations copyright © Neal Layton, 2003
The right of Frieda Wishinsky and Neal Layton to be identified as
the author and illustrator of this work has been asserted in accordance
with the Copyright, Designs and Patents Act 1988.

Picture Corgi Books are published by Random House Children's Books,
61–63 Uxbridge Road, London W5 5SA
www.**kids**at**randomhouse**.co.uk
www.**randomhouse**.co.uk
Addresses for companies within The Random House Group Limited
can be found at: www.randomhouse.co.uk/offices.htm
THE RANDOM HOUSE GROUP Limited Reg. No. 954009
A CIP catalogue record for this book is available from the British Library.

Printed in China

Jennifer Jones Won't Leave Me Alone

Frieda Wishinsky ✿ **Neal Layton**

PICTURE CORGI

Jennifer Jones won't leave me alone.
She sits by my side.
She **SHOUTS** in my ear.

She tells me she loves me.
She calls me her 'dear'.

She writes me love poems
Full of words like **adore**
Then she sticks on red hearts
She bought at the store.

And my friends laugh and snicker.
They point and they stare.
They say,

WELL, WE DON'T AND I HATE IT!

I've had quite enough.
I wish that she'd move
And take all her stuff.

She could move to the jungle
And live in a tree

And talk to the monkeys,
Instead of to me.

But if she insists
That she's not going there,

She could head for the Arctic
And bother a bear.

Or fly to
the desert

Or go to the moon.

I really don't care,
As long as it's soon.

Hurrah! Hallelujah!

Guess what I just heard?
Jennifer's moving.
Her mum's been transferred.

'I'll miss you,'
She said with a
tear in her eye.
Then she gave me
a kiss
And whispered,

'Goodbye'.

Now her seat is all empty.
There's nobody there.
There's no one to kiss me.

There's no one to care.

So I write in my notebook.
I add and subtract.
I study my spelling.
I learn a new fact.

But it's boring! It's lonely!
I miss her a lot.
I wish she'd return

To her usual spot .

And to make matters worse
She writes:

It's divine
Seeing Paris at night,

Munching chocolates
in Brussels,

Eating pizza
in Rome,

Nibbling viennese pastries you can't get at home.

Percy Lubbock, Esqu

Emmetts

Oh, she's having such fun,
I thought in despair.

She'll never come home.
She'll stay over there.

But then I read on,
'I'll see you in June.'

And I yelled,

WHOOP-DEE-DOO!!!

She'll return very soon.'

And as soon as I did,
The kids wondered why
I was jumping and shouting.
So I thought,

But I told them the truth
As I opened the door,
And I ran off to buy

Red hearts
at the store.

Here are some books we think you'll *love* . . .

One Kiss, One Hug

By Jason Chapman

Traction Man and the Beach Odyssey

By Mini Grey

The Boy Who Cried Ninja

By Alex Latimer

Good Little Wolf

By Nadia Shireen

Dog Loves Books

By Louise Yates

For more great books visit:
www.kidsatrandomhouse.co.uk